Cool kids know

About honeybees and where honey comes from

The home of the honeybee is called a hive.

The hive is made of wood and has a metal roof.

hive

The traditional hive was made of twisted straw.

We call this a skep.

skep

In the hive, you will find thousands of bees.

The majority of the bees are called worker bees.

The worker bees are the smallest in the hive.

honeybee

There is only one
Queen Bee
in a hive.

She is the biggest bee in the hive.

She has a long body and she only
leaves the hive when she
is looking for a new home.

The Queen Bee is the
mother of all the
bees in the hive.

The boy bees are called drones.

They are bigger than the worker bees
but smaller than the Queen Bee.

drone

The hive is a clean and organised home.

On wooden frames, the honeybees build
identical
small rooms made of wax.

The rooms are called cells.

In the cells, you can find small eggs
that will become
honeybees.

We can also find larvae.

The worker bees take care of
each larva until it grows
big and strong
and it is ready to
transform into a bee.

Some cells are used to store pollen.

The pollen is collected from flowers.
The pollen is the food
loved by the small
larvae.

Most of the cells are used
to store the sweet
honey.

From spring to autumn, the honeybees travel every day in search of flowers.

From each flower, the honeybees collect
pollen and nectar.

In return for what the flowers give
to them, the honeybees help pollinate
the flowers.

Pollination is the process that helps flowers
to make seeds and
baby plants.

Honeybees carry the nectar in
their stomachs and
the pollen
on their legs.
They look like golden jewels.

The person taking care of the bees is called a beekeeper.

The beekeeper is the one who collects the honey.

A good beekeeper does not take all the honey from beehive.

They also make sure to give the bees more food over the winter.

The cells full of honey collected from
the hive
make the honeycomb.

After taking out the honey from
the honeycomb we are left
with wax.

We can use the wax to make candles.

Beeswax has many other uses.

Honey is a natural sugar made
from the nectar collected by
the bees from flowers.

It is good for you to eat.

It helps people feel better and can
be used as medicine.

And so now you know all about honeybees
and where honey
comes from.

9 781068 659300